LITTLE RED RIDING HOOD

FAY'S FAIRY TALES

LITTLE RED RIDING HOOD

WILLIAM WEGMAN

WITH CAROLE KISMARIC AND MARVIN HEIFERMAN

SCHOLASTIC INC.
NEW YORK TORONTO LONDON AUCKLAND SYDNEY

There was once a little girl who lived with her mother and father in a small wooden house by the edge of the forest. Everyone was fond of this girl, but she was without question most dear to her grandmother, who lived in a cottage across the great meadow at the far end of the woods. Her grandmother loved making the little girl special things to wear, the most beautiful being a red-velvet hooded cloak that the girl always wore when she went out. Because of this everyone called her Little Red Riding Hood — even her mother and father.

One morning Little Red Riding Hood and her mother baked blueberry muffins. They each ate one. Her mother put the rest in a basket and said, "Bring this basket to your grandmother. She hasn't been feeling well, and your visit will cheer her up."

"Bring this basket to your grandmother."

"Don't worry."

"Oh dear," said Little Red Riding Hood in dismay. "Poor Grand-mother."

"You must go straight there and return home before dark," said her mother. "Do not dawdle."

"Don't worry," said Little Red Riding Hood. But her mother did worry as she watched her little girl disappear from view.

Little Red Riding Hood loved going to Grandmother's house. It was such a pretty walk. I will pick Grandmother a beautiful bouquet of flowers from the great meadow, she thought as she turned off the road onto the path that led to the big field with all the daisies.

Wildflowers bloomed...

...all around.

I will pick Grandmother a beautiful bouquet.

Wildflowers bloomed all around. "Some of these will be nice. Oh, and over there, some of *those*," she said. "Grandmother will feel so much better when she sees these. They smell really nice, like talcum powder with honey."

Little Red Riding Hood knew many routes to her grandmother's house, and she often let whimsy decide which path to take. Perhaps she would cut diagonally across the meadow and walk directly through the woods today. She knew the forest well and loved its aura of enchantment. Or she might stop and visit her friend the woodsman, who lived in a cabin just at the edge of the forest. They could chat if he was home. She could watch him chop wood and help him stack it. Maybe she could use the small ax and help him trim branches. But, remembering her mission and her mother's admonition, she decided that this was not prudent today. She would just say hello.

"Hello, Little Red Riding Hood," greeted the woodsman cheerfully.

"Hello, Woodsman," said Little Red Riding Hood. "I'm sorry; my grandmother is ill, so I can't help you today. I am bringing her a basket of muffins. I had better be going now."

"Well, you'd better," replied the woodsman. "And give your grandmother my regards. Wish her a speedy recovery."

"I will," promised Little Red Riding Hood, and she continued on her way.

"I had better be going now."

A few hundred steps past the woodsman's cabin she entered the forest. Soon she heard a hooting sound. *Hoot. Hoot. Hoot. Hoot.* It was just an owl. She wasn't even a little afraid. "Hello, owl," she said.

I wonder who planted this forest, she thought, gazing up at the towering trees. It must have been long ago. The woodsman will know. I'll ask him on my way back.

"Look, a deer. It has antlers. It must be a stag. Hello, stag," she whispered to herself so as not to startle it.

She wasn't even a little afraid.

"Hello, Little Red Riding Hood," a muffled voice replied. But when Little Red Riding Hood turned around there was nothing there.

"Hello, Little Red Riding Hood." This time the voice was right behind her. She turned around and again saw nothing.

All of a sudden a very big wolf popped out from behind a cedar tree. "Hello, Little Red Riding Hood. Where are you going today, and what is in your basket?"

"Muffins for my grandmother. She is ill, and I must go to her straightaway."

...there was nothing there.

The wolf could barely contain his glee. "What kind of muffins?" he asked.

"Blueberry," she answered innocently.

Overcoming his almost overpowering urge to eat her *and* the muffins on the spot, the wolf thought, If I can detour this young thing for a few precious moments, I can have the grandmother, too. Then I will have the blueberry muffins, and for dessert I will eat sweet Little Red Riding Hood.

"Your grandmother lives in the south woods of the great forest, does she not?" the wolf asked.

"Why, no, Mr. Wolf, she has the old cottage at the edge of the north woods."

"Oh *that* grandmother! Little Red Riding Hood, come this way," said the wolf. "I want to show you something I think your grandmother will appreciate. She likes flowers, doesn't she?"

"Oh, yes," replied Little Red Riding Hood. "I have picked her a bouquet from the meadow."

"Hello, Little Red Riding Hood."

"But those are so mundane," he said haughtily. "Anybody could give that. Wouldn't you like to bring her something *really* special? I know where you can pick some anemones, flowers especially cherished by grandmothers and particularly harmonious with the blueberry type of muffin. A perfect complement to those weeds you have already picked. Follow me a ways. Not far, not far at all...this way," he said, leading her down the forest road to a fork. "Take this path a little farther and you will find a small stand of trees. Within that grove are the flowers beloved by grandmothers universally."

"Really?" asked Little Red Riding Hood.

"Truly," replied the wolf.

The wolf slinked off in the other direction.

"It is I, Little Red Riding Hood."

So Little Red Riding Hood set off to find the special flowers, and the wolf slinked off in the other direction. Moving swiftly and smoothly through the dense forest bramble, the wolf arrived, panting and salivating, at Grandmother's house in only a matter of minutes. He crept up onto the shallow porch, being extra careful not to disturb any of the deck furniture, and knocked on the door.

"Who is it?" the grandmother asked weakly.

"It is I, Little Red Riding Hood," answered the wolf in a strained voice. "I have brought you some blueberry muffins."

"Come right in, dear," said the grandmother. "You know my door is never locked. Do you have a cold? Your voice sounds hoarse."

With that, the wolf barged in and gobbled up the grandmother whole. Then the wolf disguised himself in Grandmother's nightshirt and dressing gown. The process of transformation amused him immensely. He played with her sleeping bonnet in front of the mirror and applied rouge to his jowls.

"Hello, Little Red Riding Hood," he said, rehearsing his lines. "I'm so happy to see you. So good of you to come. Hello, Little Red, so glad you could bring me a little snack. Muffins are they? My little muffin, my little red muffin, my little red-hooded muffin."

The process of transformation amused him immensely.

He rushed over to the window.

Hearing the sound of a child whistling, he rushed over to the window and saw Little Red Riding Hood approaching the front door. Quickly, he put on Grandmother's bifocal glasses and leapt onto the bed, covering most of himself with blankets, and waited for her knock on the door. He did not have long to wait.

Knock, knock, knock.

"Who is it? Oh, Little Red Riding Hood? Come right in, dear. You know my door is never locked."

Little Red Riding Hood felt a chill as she entered the house. Something was different. The sight of her beloved grandmother startled her.

Something was different.

"Come closer."

"Grandmother," she said, "you look different." Approaching, she looked closer. Her grandmother's ears seemed unusually large. "What big ears you have!" she exclaimed.

"All the better to hear you with, my dear. Come closer, and I'll let you touch them."

Stepping closer, Little Red Riding Hood noticed that her grandmother's nose seemed huge. Perhaps it was because of her condition. "Grandmother, what a big nose you have!" she exclaimed.

"All the better to smell you with, my dear sweet morsel. Come closer still so I can give you a little kiss," said the wolf, smiling.

"Come closer still."

Obediently, she came closer. "Grandmother, what big teeth you have...," she stammered.

"All the better to eat you with, my dear!" snarled the wolf, baring his enormous fangs.

And with this, the wolf sprang from the bed and devoured the little girl in one amazing gulp. Sated and feeling no remorse, the gluttonous wolf groaned with pleasure and soon fell fast asleep.

"All the better to eat you with, my dear!"

Meanwhile, the woodsman became concerned that Little Red Riding Hood had not yet stopped by on her way back home. He decided to check in on her at the house of her grandmother.

At Grandmother's house, the woodsman peeked in the window before entering. He could not quite discern what was upon Grandmother's bed. It looked more like a wolf than a person, but it was bigger than a wolf. It was bigger than a person, too. He found the door open and went in, and seeing it was indeed a wolf, he reached for his rifle to shoot. But where were Little Red Riding Hood and her grandmother? He looked everywhere before he realized what had happened. Not wanting harm to befall them, the woodsman paused.

Before the woodsman could decide what action to take, the wolf awoke, yawning and groaning after his recent meal. He stretched his furry limbs, popping a button off Grandmother's nightgown, and opened his eyes. The sudden shock of seeing the armed woodsman made him quite nauseous. He felt dizzy and threw up. Out flew Little Red Riding Hood and her grandmother, both still very much alive.

"He felt dizzy."

"Oh dear!" exclaimed Little Red Riding Hood. "What happened?"

"Thank you, Woodsman," said Grandmother gratefully. "You saved our lives!"

They all hugged one another and danced around the room in glee. The wolf, taking advantage of the commotion, slipped out the back door and headed for the bramble.

After cleaning up, Little Red Riding Hood's grandmother made chocolate cupcakes with silver candies. Then Grandmother, the woodsman, and Little Red Riding Hood had themselves a party with colorful balloons and ribbons, but they were too upset to eat. One of the balloons broke free and landed on a candle, exploding with a loud bang and causing quite a fright. Other than that, nothing bad happened.

Grandmother made chocolate cupcakes.

EPILOGUE

The following week, Little Red Riding Hood returned to her grandmother's house to bring her a basket of fruit. She went straight there, as her mother told her to. She did not dawdle or stray.

Again Little Red Riding Hood and her grandmother were visited by the wolf, but this time they did not let him in. The wolf eventually gave up and went somewhere else.

To my sister, Pam

ISBN 0-590-13198-2

Text and Photographs copyright © 1993
by William Wegman.
All rights reserved. Published by Scholastic Inc.,
555 Broadway, New York, NY 10012, by arrangement
with Hyperion Books for Children.

12 11 10 9 8 7 6 5 4 3 2 1   6 7 8 9/9 0 1/0

Printed in the U.S.A.   14

First Scholastic printing, October 1996

This book is set in 14-point Adroit Light.

ACKNOWLEDGMENTS

With thanks to Stan Bartash, Andrea Beeman, Mr. and
Mrs. William Booker, Jason Burch, Christine Burgin,
Hilary Coolidge, Stacy Fischer, Fran Griscom, Ed
and Ellen Halle, Leslie Hendricks, Arnold and Pam
Lehman, Dave McMillan, The Pace/MacGill Gal-
lery, John Reuter, Tracy Storer, Lloyd and Elizabeth
Volckening, Pam Wegman, and Fran York.

LITTLE RED RIDING HOOD was developed and edited
by William Wegman with Marvin Heiferman and Carole
Kismaric/Lookout Books, New York.